The Littles

Go to School

by John Peterson
Illustrated by Roberta Carter Clark
Cover illustration by Jacqueline Rogers

A
LITTLE APPLE
PAPERBACK

SCHOLASTIC INC.

New York   Toronto   London   Auckland   Sydney

ISBN 0-590-42129-8

Copyright © 1983 by John Peterson.
Illustrations copyright © 1983 by Scholastic Inc.
All rights reserved. Published by Scholastic Inc.
APPLE PAPERBACKS is a registered trademark of Scholastic Inc.

48 47 46 45 44 43 42 41 40 39   4 5 6 7 8 9/0

Printed in the U.S.A.   40

To
Carl and Emily

The Littles Go to School

Tom Little and his sister, Lucy, got as close to Henry Bigg's desk as they could. They didn't want to miss anything.

Henry didn't know that ten-year-old Tom and eight-year-old Lucy were watching him do his homework. They stayed hidden in a lookout place next to Henry's desk.

Tom and Lucy could hide in very small places because they were tiny. Everyone in their family was tiny. Their father was the tallest Little, and he was only six inches tall.

The tiny Little family lived in the same house with regular-sized people—the George W. Bigg family. The Littles were so small that all nine members had plenty of room in their secret ten-room apartment in one wall of the house. The Biggs had no idea they were living there.

"What's Henry doing now?" whispered Lucy.

"I'm not sure—I can't see," said Tom. "It's a book report, I think. He keeps looking at that book. I'm pretty sure it's a storybook instead of a schoolbook."

"Tom, I know that Henry has a book report outline his teacher gave him," said Lucy. "I *have* to see it. I can't do *my* book report unless I do."

"Then we'll have to get up higher," Tom said. "Then maybe we can see over his shoulder."

Suddenly Henry got up. He went to the door of his room. "Hey, Mom!" he yelled. "Can I stop now? It's already eight-thirty. I want to see *Starship Nova* on TV."

"Did you finish your homework?" Mrs. Bigg answered.

"I only have a little more to do," Henry yelled. "I can finish my book report tomorrow. I have a study period first thing."

"Henry, are you *sure* you'll have time?"

"Sure I'm sure," Henry said. He was already in the hall and heading downstairs for the living room.

Tom jumped up. "C'mon, Lucy!" he said. He ran across a table and leaped the three inches over to Henry's desk. Lucy ran after him.

Tom began pulling loose papers out of Henry's green folder. "The book report outline is in here, I'll bet," he said. "Here it is, Lucy! You'll have to memorize it."

Lucy stood on the book report outline and looked down at the words. "*Name of Book* is first," she said. "Then *Author, Type of Book, Main Characters, Conflict* and *Resolution*. Tom! What do all those big words mean?"

"Just memorize them, Lucy," said Tom. "We'll find out what they mean later."

Just then the children heard Henry Bigg coming back up the stairs. He was talking to himself. "For crying out loud!" he said. "I can straighten out my desk *after* the program."

It was too late for Tom and Lucy to get off the desk. "Quick, Lucy!" said Tom. He dived into an open drawer.

Lucy jumped in after her brother.

"Over here!" Tom whispered. "Behind these baseball cards."

The tiny children crouched in the dark drawer. They heard Henry shuffling papers and books. He complained all the while. "I don't see why we have to do so much homework," he said. "Dumb teachers, anyway!"

"Tom!" whispered Lucy. "What if Henry closes the drawer?"

"Oh, oh!" said Tom. "I didn't think of that."

But Tom and Lucy were lucky that day. Henry did his usual sloppy cleanup job and forgot to close the desk drawer. He did, however, stuff some papers into the drawer on top of the tiny children.

After Henry was gone, Tom and Lucy pushed the papers aside and climbed out of the drawer.

"I wish Henry didn't hate homework so much," said Lucy.

"Yeah," said Tom. "It would make it a lot easier for us to do our schoolwork if he spent more time on his."

"The big kids in Tina Small's house are good students," Lucy said. "She says she learns a lot."

"I wish Henry would work on his ocean report for science," said Tom. "I love the ocean."

"He hasn't worked on that for two weeks," said Lucy.

"I'm going to make a report just like it," said Tom.

"Tom, we're not supposed to *copy* the big children," said Lucy. "Remember, our teacher said we're supposed to do something *like* what Henry does, but not the same thing."

"I know, I know," said Tom, "but I like the ocean."

"Well, the teacher is coming to visit us this week," Lucy said. "Why don't you ask her if you can do it?"

"I should have thought of something," said Tom. "I told her I would have a science report ready when she came again. I don't even have a good idea yet. Now it's too late."

It was lunchtime the next day. The Littles were in the kitchen of their apartment in the wall of the Biggs' house. The whole family was there—Tom and Lucy; their parents, Mr. and Mrs. William T. Little; their baby sister, Betsy; Granny and Grandpa Little; Uncle Nick; and Uncle Pete.

The Littles were not the only tiny family in the Big Valley. There were tiny people living in the woods; other families who lived in cozy burrows under the ground and in trees; and even tinies who lived in the town dump. Tiny people like the Littles who lived with big people called themselves House Tinies.

TOM   LUCY   MR. LITTLE

All tiny people had tails. In every other way they looked like very small ordinary people. Their tails were good-looking. The tiny people were proud of them and always kept them well brushed.

An amazing thing about the tiny people was that no big person had ever seen one of them. The tinies didn't trust big people, even though they were fond of some of them.

Tiny people were fast and clever. Every House Tiny worked hard at knowing the best hiding places in the house he lived in. And there were secret doors too. Mrs. Little had picked up their lunch of leftovers by using the electric-socket door on the kitchen counter.

MRS. LITTLE   BABY BETSY   GRANNY

UNCLE PETE   UNCLE NICK   GRANDPA

As the Littles were sitting around their kitchen table, Mr. Little said: "Well, Tom, I've been telling you that you had better get going on your schoolwork. Now your teacher is coming and you're late."

Tom looked down. "I'm sorry, Dad."

"Why don't you let the boy be," said Granny Little. "You know very well, William, that tiny children are allowed to learn whatever they wish to learn after they've learned their reading, writing, and arithmetic. And they can learn just as fast or as slow as they want to."

"It's a silly way of teaching children, if you ask me," said Uncle Nick.

Granny Little laughed. "I suppose they do it better at the town dump."

DELLA   AND   DINKY

Uncle Nick was a retired major in the Mouse Force Brigade. He had been a soldier for thirty years fighting mice in Trash City. (This was the tiny people's city in the town dump.)

"As far as I can see, it *is* done better at Trash City," said Uncle Nick. "They have a regular school and teachers. The children are in school from eight in the morning until three in the afternoon."

"Well, of course we can't do that," said Mr. Little. "House tinies are too far apart for that to work. The best we can do is send them to the big children's school for a week. Their teacher, Miss Beta Gogg, does an excellent job with them there."

"One week seems hardly worth the effort," said Uncle Nick.

"That's what *I* think!" said Lucy.

"Now, Lucy," said Mr. Little. "We've been over this a thousand times. You know the rules. All the tiny children over eight have to go to the school for at least a week after the big children are finished for the year."

"But I've never been!" Lucy said. Her lip trembled. "I'm afraid."

"Oh, Lucy, there's nothing to be afraid of," said Tom.

"Weren't *you* afraid the first time you went?" Lucy asked.

"Well, I suppose...a little," Tom said. "But, really, Lucy, there's nothing to it."

"I still don't see why I have to go," said Lucy. "Miss Gogg comes to see us every month, and we learn lots of stuff on our own."

"But, Lucy, it's fun too," said Tom. "You get to see lots of the tiny kids from all over the Big Valley. We use the chalk-boards. We read some of the textbooks the big kids use. There are maps and charts, and we live in dormitories in the walls of the classroom. You'll like it."

"I'll bet!" said Lucy. She made a face.

Mrs. Little put her arm around Lucy. "Your teacher is very fond of you, Lucy. She knows that some of the new students are worried about going to school."

Mr. Little nodded his head. "Miss

Gogg will watch out for you, Lucy," he said.

"We are very lucky to have a teacher who is intelligent and well informed," said Mrs. Little.

"Miss Gogg ought to be well informed," said Mr. Little. "She has lived in the walls of the school for years and years."

"When is she coming to see you?" asked Uncle Nick.

"This week," said Tom.

"Cousin Dinky and Della are flying her in their glider from house to house," said Mr. Little. "She'll stay two days, as usual."

Uncle Nick shook his head. "I still say two days a month doesn't seem like enough time to get any real teaching done," he said.

"Well, it always has been enough time," said Mrs. Little. "Miss Gogg goes over what Tom and Lucy have done since she was here last. Then they talk about what they'll do for the next month."

A few days later Tom and Lucy took the elevator up to the attic. The Littles had made the elevator from a soup can and some pulleys and string. It went up and down inside the walls of the house.

On the way up, Lucy said, "I love my new book report. It's perfect."

"Lucy, you shouldn't brag," said Tom.

"I learned what all those big words mean from Grandpa," Lucy said. "Did you know that *resolution* means 'how things turned out in the end'?"

"I think so," said Tom. "Anyway, that reminds me: I wish there was a *resolution* to my problem about what to do a science report on."

"Miss Gogg will give you a good idea," said Lucy. "Wait and see."

The elevator stopped at the attic, and Tom and Lucy got off.

"I saw some notepaper up here," said Tom. He searched through some cardboard boxes. "It had the Biggs' address at the top."

"That's just what I want," said Lucy. She carried a pencil over her shoulder.

"You really don't need to write this letter," said Tom. He sat down on a picture frame. "Your book report is good. Miss Gogg will like it."

"I'm not doing this for Miss Gogg," said Lucy. "I just want to do it."

"Oh? I thought you wanted to do extra work for Miss Gogg because you're afraid of her," said Tom.

"She is kind of tough," Lucy said. "But I'm not afraid of her. What I'm really afraid of is going to the big kids' school."

"That's cuckoo—do you know that, Lucy?" said Tom. "*Everyone* in the family thinks you're being silly about going to school."

"I don't care," said Lucy. "I'm still scared."

"*I* can hardly wait to go," Tom said.

"Tom, can we find the notepaper so I can write the letter?" said Lucy. "I *hate* talking about going to school. It gives me goose bumps."

Tom stood up. He pointed across the attic floor. "There it is!" he said. "That's the box. I told you it was around here someplace."

In a few moments the tiny children had a piece of the Biggs' notepaper on the floor.

"I don't know how you're going to do this," Tom said. He sat cross-legged on the paper and watched his sister.

Lucy held the large pencil in her two hands. She stood on top of the paper. "I'll write just as I always do," she said, "only I'll write lots larger."

"What are you going to say?" said Tom.

"First I'll say: 'Dear Mrs. Rice' — she's the author — 'Your book, *We Lived With Giants*, is wonderful.' Then I'll tell her that I *love* to read about giants," said Lucy. "And that I wish there really were giants."

Tom laughed. "Well, there really *are* giants," he said.

"No there aren't, Tom. You're fooling."

"The Biggs are giants," Tom went on.

"Oh, Tom, that's silly!" said Lucy. "They're regular-sized people. I heard Daddy say so lots of times."

"They sure look like giants to me," said Tom. "You and I could easily fit in Henry's hand."

"That's because we're *tiny* people," Lucy said.

Tom shook his head. "Lucy, don't you understand? A person who is big enough to hold Henry Bigg in the palm of his hand would be a giant to Henry. But Henry could hold *us* in the palm of *his* hand. That makes Henry a giant to us."

"Oh, I get it!" Lucy said. "That's right." She thought for a moment. "Hey, Tom, if Mrs. Rice is good at writing about giants and regular-sized people, maybe she'd like to write a story about regular-sized people and *tiny* people."

"Maybe," said Tom.

"I've decided," Lucy said. "*That's* what I'm going to say in my letter to her."

Lucy found that holding the pencil with two hands and writing large letters was hard to do. She ruined two pieces of the Biggs' notepaper trying to write *Dear*

Mrs. Rice. Finally, with Tom's help, she wrote the letter.

At the end, Lucy wrote: *And be sure the tiny people have tails. They will look better with them. I'm sure if there really were tiny people, they would have tails.*

"There," said Lucy. "It's finished. Now I'll sign Henry's name."

"It's too bad you can't sign your own name," said Tom.

""If I did, we'd never get a letter back," Lucy said. She smiled. "Golly, won't Henry be surprised!"

"Come on, Lucy," said Tom. "Let's put it in an envelope. We've just got time to get it in the Biggs' mailbox for the afternoon mail pickup."

The day finally came for Miss Beta Gogg to visit the Littles. The whole family was on the roof of the Biggs' house waiting to greet her. They were watching the sky, looking for Cousin Dinky's glider.

Cousin Dinky Little and his wife, Della, didn't live with the Littles, but they often visited them. They carried the mail back and forth among the tiny families. The two glider pilots loved to fly up and down the Big Valley having adventures. One of their regular jobs was to fly Miss Gogg from house to house so that she could visit the tiny children.

Mr. Little pointed to a small flag hanging from the TV antenna. "According to the flag, the wind is blowing from the northeast," he said. "They'll probably come from there."

Tom and Lucy had climbed up on top of the chimney to see better.

"There she is!" yelled Lucy.

Everyone looked up. They saw the glider speeding toward the roof. It was coming in high. A gust of wind carried it past the house.

"Turn around!" Tom yelled.

As if on Tom's command, the glider banked and turned in the sky. It drifted down toward the roof. As it got near, two parachutes snapped open. They acted like brakes, slowing the glider down.

A fishhook tied to a piece of twine fell from the glider. As the glider landed on the roof, this fishhook anchor caught on a shingle. The twine pulled taut, and the glider came to a stop.

In a few moments Cousin Dinky, Della, and Miss Beta Gogg were out of the cockpit, saying hello to the Littles.

"Sorry about that landing," said Cousin Dinky. "I was busy explaining the controls to Miss Gogg, and we flew right on by."

Della stood next to Miss Gogg. "Dinky is trying to talk Miss Gogg into learning how to fly," she said.

Miss Gogg shook hands with Tom and Lucy.

"Thomas, how are you?" she said. "And Lucy, you look splendid! Did both of you watch the landing closely?"

"I did!" Tom said.

"I think I did," said Lucy.

"Then tell me," said Miss Gogg. "What did your cousin do to turn the glider around after we flew past the roof?"

"He banked it to the right," said Tom.

"And how did he do that, Thomas?" asked Miss Gogg.

"He pushed the stick to the right," said Tom.

"Of course," said Miss Gogg. "But what does that do, exactly?"

"It raises the right aileron and lowers the left aileron," Tom went on.

"And what does *that* do?" Miss Gogg asked.

"I'm not sure," said Tom.

"Think about it, Thomas," said Miss Gogg, "and tell me later."

Cousin Dinky put his arm around Mrs.

Little. "I'm starved, Auntie," he said. "Is it too early to ask you what wonderful things Mrs. Bigg is serving for dinner this evening?"

Later, after dinner, Tom and Lucy had their lesson with Miss Gogg. "Lucy," she said, "I've never read your favorite book, *We Lived With Giants*. But your report was so interesting it made me want to."

Lucy smiled. "It was one of Henry's books," she said. "So he helped me, I guess. And Tom helped a lot! Especially with the letter to the author, Mrs. Rice."

"I'm looking forward to her answer," Miss Gogg said. "I hope you will share what she says with the other students when you come to school this year."

When Lucy heard the word *school*, she stopped smiling, and her head drooped.

Tom tried to change the subject. He said, "Miss Gogg, would you like to see the Biggs' animals? I have nothing to do right now. I'll show them to you."

"What animals do the Biggs have?" Miss Gogg asked.

"A cat, a bird, three gerbils, and six chickens," said Tom.

"Thomas, I have a thought," said Miss Gogg. "You wanted a science report idea. Why don't you and Lucy work together on one about the Biggs' animals? It could be the last school report of the year for both of you."

"I'd like that!" said Lucy. She was smiling again.

For the next few weeks, Tom and Lucy worked on their science report on the Biggs' animals.

Hildy, the cat, was no problem for them. Tom had tamed the cat a long time ago, and the children already knew a lot about her.

The chickens were behind the Biggs' house. They lived in a fenced-off part of the yard where there was a henhouse. Mostly, Tom and Lucy studied the chickens from the Biggs' roof. They used Mr. Bigg's binoculars, which they managed to borrow once in a while. They made one trip to the henhouse to count the eggs and to see how the hens roosted.

Henry Bigg's bird was a parakeet. The cage was in his room near the window. On a shelf nearby were the gerbils and their cage.

Tom and Lucy came to Henry's room every morning after he left for school. They knew how to open both cage doors. They spent some time in each cage every morning.

The parakeet didn't mind having the tiny children near. The gerbils seemed to actually enjoy the visits.

After a while, Tom and Lucy decided to teach one of the gerbils some tricks. They showed the animal what they wanted it to do.

Lucy said, "Roll over!" to Tom. He lay down in the wood chips at the bottom of the cage and rolled over.

The gerbil watched Tom closely.

Then Lucy said, "Sit up!", and Tom sat up for her.

After the demonstration, the gerbil came up to Tom and sniffed him all over.

"Now it's your turn," Tom said to the gerbil. "Roll over!"

The gerbil ran around in circles.

"Sit up!" Tom commanded.

The gerbil sat down and scratched itself.

They tried this method a number of times, then Lucy said, "Oh, Tom, he's never going to do anything we tell him, is he?" She sat down in the wood chips and leaned against the bars of the cage.

"Henry's book on gerbils says he *can* learn tricks," Tom said.

"Let's not try anymore," said Lucy. "Let's finish our report. We have enough information without teaching the gerbils tricks." Then she said, "Tom, do you think Mother and Dad will force me to go to school?"

"Sure they will," Tom said. "It's for your own good."

"Forcing people," said Lucy, "is like *kidnapping* them."

"One way or the other," said Tom, "you'll have to go to sch—"

All of a sudden the tiny children heard footsteps coming down the hall.

"Tom!" said Lucy. She jumped up. "Is that Henry?"

"He's in school," said Tom. He ran toward the cage door.

Whoever was coming stopped at the bedroom door. The knob clicked, and the door started to open.

"Quick, Lucy!" whispered Tom. "Under the wood chips."

The children dove into a corner of the cage and dug themselves into the wood chips as far as they could go.

It was Mrs. Bigg.

She came into the bedroom and walked straight to the gerbils' cage. "You're going on a trip today, little fellows," said Mrs. Bigg.

She picked up the cage, left the room, and went downstairs and out the door.

Tom and Lucy were lying side by side in the wood chips at the bottom of the cage.

"Tom!" whispered Lucy. "What'll we do?"

"Be quiet!" whispered Tom. "And don't move!"

Mrs. Bigg placed the gerbils' cage in the front seat of her car. She drove out of the driveway and down the road.

Tom and Lucy lay very still under the wood chips. After a while Tom stuck his head up to look around. He saw Mrs. Bigg in the driver's seat. She might see them if they tried to get out of the cage.

Finally, the car stopped.

Mrs. Bigg picked up the cage and took it into a building. She carried it up some stairs and into a room.

Tom and Lucy heard the voices of many children.

They heard a woman say, "Children, Mrs. Bigg has brought Henry's gerbils to visit us for a few days."

Mrs. Bigg said, "Henry was in this class four years ago. He remembered that the children liked to have animals in the classroom. He insisted that I bring the gerbils for your last week before summer vacation."

"Tom!" whispered Lucy. "Where are we?"

"Did she say 'classroom'?" Tom asked.

"I think so," said Lucy.

Tom raised his head out of the wood chips for a moment. "It is!" he said. "We're in *school*!"

"School?" said Lucy. "I don't want to be in school!"

By this time, Mrs. Bigg was through talking to the second-grade teacher and had left the room.

"All right, children," said the teacher. "You may gather around the gerbils' cage for a few minutes."

The children dashed from their seats and formed a half-circle around the table where the cage was. They made all kinds of comments.

"Mrs. White, can we touch them?"

"Oh, look! They're so cute!"

"Yuk — they look like little *rats!*"

"*We* have hamsters in *our* house."

"What do they eat?"

"Children, if you'll be quiet I'll tell you something about these little animals," said the teacher, Mrs. White.

Tom and Lucy were so scared they had almost stopped breathing. Lucy moved her hand slowly through the wood chips and found Tom's hand. She held it hard.

For the next few minutes the teacher told the children what she knew about gerbils. She reached into the cage and picked up one of the animals so the children could pet it.

"They'll be here for a part of the week," Mrs. White said, "so you will get a chance to know them better. Now, let's all get back to our work."

When the children were back in their seats, Lucy whispered to Tom, "If the gerbils are going to stay here, how do we get back home?"

"I don't know," said Tom, "but we can't stay in this cage and wait for Mrs. Bigg."

"What'll we do?"

"We can go to Miss Gogg's apartment," Tom said. "She must be there by now. *Someone* must be there."

"Do you know the way?"

"Yes," said Tom. "But the trouble is, the secret door into the wall passageway is at the other end of the room."

"Tom! How do we get there?" said Lucy. "There are *thousands* of big children all over the room."

"I have a plan," said Tom. He started to get up. "Follow me."

Just then the schoolroom door opened, and a woman came in. She said hello to Mrs. White and walked toward the back of the room.

Tom ducked down into the wood chips. "Stay hidden!" he said to Lucy.

The woman sat right down at the table next to the gerbils' cage.

"Darn!" whispered Tom.

In a few moments a child came over and sat down at the table with the woman. "What are you going to read for me today, Jenny?" said the woman.

The child held up a book for the woman to see. "This," she said. "It's about a mean kid named Max, and how he picks on this kid named Tony, and what happens and everything."

Poor Tom and Lucy. They had to lie under those wood chips and listen to children read stories. Some of them were good stories. But it was hard to enjoy them while lying facedown in a pile of wood chips — only inches away from big people.

About an hour went by, and finally the woman got up. As she left the table, Tom hopped up. "C'mon, Lucy!" he said. "We've got to get out of here."

The tiny children ran from the cage and hid behind a terrarium on the table.

Tom pointed to a bookshelf next to the table. "We've got to jump from this table to that bookshelf," he said, "and then get as far along the shelf as we can before it happens."

"Before what happens?" asked Lucy.

Tom didn't answer. He started to run, and Lucy ran right behind him.

The tiny children dashed along the bookshelf. When they got to the end of it, they were quite close to the front of the room. They climbed down from the bookshelf to the floor.

Tom put his finger to his lips. "Sh!" he said to Lucy. Then he pointed across the room.

Lucy looked and saw a tiny person's door on the wall near the floor. It was almost invisible, as all tiny doors are. Lucy knew what to look for, though, and she spotted it.

Mrs. White was working with a reading group of six children very near the secret door. She had written some hard vocabulary words on the blackboard and was pointing to them.

"What are they waiting for?" Tom whispered. "They've had plenty of time to get out."

"Who's waiting for what?" asked Lucy.

"You'll see," Tom said. "Any minute now."

Suddenly a child at the back of the room screamed. "They're loose! The gerbils are loose!"

"That's it, Lucy!" whispered Tom. "Get ready to run for the door."

All the children rushed to the back of the room.

"There's one gerbil!" yelled a girl.

"Where?"

A scream.

"Children! Children!" It was Mrs. White.

"I got one! *Oops!* It got away."

While this was going on, Tom and Lucy ran across the floor without being seen. Tom opened the secret door, and they hurried through.

It was pitch-black in the wall passage-way.

It was twelve noon at the Littles'. Time for lunch. Mrs. Little was serving warmed-up leftovers from breakfast. "I was hoping to get us some nice leftover potato salad," she said, "but Mrs. Bigg has been out all morning."

"So we'll eat leftover oatmeal," said Granny Little. "I like it better than potato salad, anyway."

"*Umph!*" said Uncle Pete. "Oatmeal always reminds me of library paste — you know, that gooey stuff they use at school."

"I like it!" said Grandpa Little. "Oatmeal always hits the spot."

"Don't smack your lips, Amos," said Granny Little. "You'll set a bad example for the children."

"Where *are* the kids?" said Uncle Pete, looking around. "They're usually the first in line for a meal."

Grandpa Little ate and talked at the same time. "They've been... spending every morn... ing in Henry's room... *(gulp!)*... studying his gerbils."

"They should be back by now," said Mrs. Little, looking worried.

"Tom and Lucy are probably on the roof with their father and Uncle Nick," said Uncle Pete.

But just then Mr. Little and Uncle Nick came in — alone.

"Will," said Mrs. Little to her husband, "where are Tom and Lucy?"

"I don't know," said Mr. Little. "I haven't seen them for hours."

"Oh, my heavens!" Mrs. Little said. "The gerbils have attacked them."

Mr. and Mrs. Little, Uncle Pete, and

Uncle Nick raced through the wall passageways to Henry's room. The gerbils' cage was gone! No one could speak for a moment. Mrs. Little tried not to scream.

"Hold it — I remember something," said Mr. Little. "Earlier, when I was on the roof picking up the mail, Mrs. Bigg was taking *something* to the car. It *could* have been the gerbils' cage. Yes, the more I think about it, it could have been the gerbils' cage."

"Maybe the kids got caught in the cage," said Uncle Pete.

"With no time to escape," Uncle Nick said.

Mrs. Little said, "Oh, dear! Where did she go with them?"

"That's the question!" Uncle Pete said.

"Maybe she took them to the veterinarian," said Mr. Little, "at the Animal Hospital. We'll just have to wait until Mrs. Bigg gets back."

"Tom and Lucy will stay hidden somehow," said Uncle Pete to Mrs. Little.

"They're smart children," said Uncle Nick nodding his head. "They'll *never* show themselves."

But, when Mrs. Bigg returned, she didn't have the cage with her.

"There's still hope," said Mr. Little. "We'll get hold of Cousin Dinky. He and Della will be able to fly to the Animal Hospital and rescue them."

He started for the roof. Mrs. Little was crying.

"Tom! Where are the lights?" cried Lucy from inside the pitch-black wall of Mrs. White's second-grade classroom. "I can't see a thing."

"I don't know," said Tom. "They were always on before."

"Can you find the way to her apartment in the dark?" said Lucy.

"I hope so," said Tom. "It's *awful* dark in here." He reached out and touched his sister's arm.

With Tom leading, the tiny children felt their way along the wall passageway. They went very slowly.

"Ouch!" said Lucy.

"What's wrong?" asked Tom.

"I bumped my head," said Lucy.

"Boy, this is dumb!" Tom said. "If only we knew where the light switch was. Why didn't I pay attention when I was here before?"

Tom nearly tripped on some stairs going down. "I don't remember this," said Tom.

"Oh, Tom," said Lucy. "We're lost!"

"There must be another passageway around here someplace," said Tom. "I'm sure we're not supposed to go down these stairs."

"What's that?" said Lucy suddenly.

"What's what?" said Tom.

"Over there," said Lucy. "Is that a light?"

"Where?"

"There!"

"Lucy, are you *pointing*?" said Tom. "It's dark, remember? I can't see anything."

"Oh, I forgot," said Lucy. "I'll point your head in the right direction."

The tiny girl took her brother's head in her hands and turned it. "There," she said. "See that tiny light way over there? It looks like it's a hundred miles away."

"There *is* a light there," Tom said.

Tom held Lucy's hand, and they moved slowly toward the light. In no time at all they came to the place.

"It's only a tiny hole in the wall," said Lucy. "No wonder it seemed so far away."

"Now I know where we are!" whispered Tom as he went up to the hole. "It's a peephole into the sixth grade. That's Henry Bigg's class!" He put his eye to the hole. "And there he is, right in front of us!"

"Let me see," whispered Lucy. She pushed her brother away from the peephole and looked through. "It *is* Henry!" she said.

There were many secret peepholes all over the school. They were so cleverly hidden that no big person ever noticed them. This hole looked out of the left eye of George Washington's portrait.

"Hey! Henry's teacher is talking about the kids' ocean reports," said Tom. "I want to hear this. Let's listen."

The teacher was asking the children questions about the ocean. Tom knew a lot about what was in Henry's report because he had watched him work on it. When the teacher got to Henry, he asked, "How deep is the deepest part of the ocean?"

Henry looked down at his desk. He fiddled with his pencil. "Ummm, ah...let's see," he said. Henry looked up at the ceiling. He coughed; he scratched his ear.

"Go on, Henry!" whispered Tom softly. "Tell him — it's in your report."

Poor Henry. He couldn't remember the answer.

"Will you repeat the question?" Henry asked.

The teacher repeated the question.

Henry said nothing.

Suddenly Tom put his mouth up to the peephole and whispered loudly: "Six and a half miles deep!"

Henry's face lit up. "Six and a half miles deep," he said.

After he spoke, Henry turned to the boy behind him. "Thanks," he said.

"For what?" the boy asked. "I didn't do anything."

By this time Lucy was yanking at Tom's arm, trying to pull him away from the peephole. "Tom!" she said. "What are you doing? Are you crazy? They'll hear you."

"I'm sorry," Tom said. "Henry didn't know the answer and I did. I got so excited I didn't realize what I was doing."

For a long time after that, Tom and Lucy wandered through the dark passageways. They were looking for Miss Gogg's apartment. Every time Tom thought they were getting close, he turned out to be wrong.

Once they even found another secret lookout place that Tom knew nothing about. It was *inside* the intercom loudspeaker at the front of the second-grade classroom.

The tiny children could look at the room through the holes in the speaker. By now, though, it was late afternoon, and the big children had gone home.

"Tom," said Lucy, "what are we going to do?"

"We must be walking in circles," said Tom.

"Mother and Dad must be awfully worried about us," said Lucy.

"We have to keep trying," said Tom. He turned. "Let's go."

After another hour of searching, they found one more tiny door. Tom pushed it open. It wasn't Miss Gogg's apartment — just another classroom.

By this time the sun had set. It was dark in the classroom, and the two children could see just enough to move around. Some moonlight and the light from a nearby streetlight came through the windows. Tom looked around, trying to figure out what room they were in.

Suddenly Lucy stopped. She stood absolutely still.

"Tom! What's that?"

A beam of moonlight fell across the wall above them. In the light Tom saw a

huge, hairy monster. Its mouth was open;
sharp teeth gleamed.

Lucy screamed, but Tom laughed!

"It's the book report monster," he said.
"*Now* I know where we are."

"Oh, Tom!" said Lucy. "It looks so
real!"

Tom pointed. "It's just a poster," he
said.

"It's stupid," said Lucy. "Why do they
want to scare somebody?"

"It's kind of a joke," Tom said. Then he read the words on the poster: "I AM VERY HUNGRY! I LIKE TO EAT BOOK REPORTS. READ A BOOK. FILL OUT A REPORT AND *FEED ME!* See — you put your book report in the monster's mouth."

"Do big kids like to do that?" said Lucy. "I wouldn't."

"Anyway," said Tom, "now I know where we are. This is Mrs. Robenki's third-grade class." He turned to his sister. "It's the room you'll be in, Lucy."

"Not me," said Lucy. "I'm not coming to a place where they think it's fun to scare you to death."

"Don't be silly, Lucy," said Tom. "C'mon. I'll show you around the room. You'll like it, honest."

"That's what *you* think!" said Lucy.

Tom led Lucy to a table with a huge ball on it. "That's a globe, Lucy," Tom said. "It's what the world looks like — only smaller."

"It looks pretty big to me," said Lucy.

Tom reached up with both hands and pushed the globe, making it spin. "Here comes South America."

Lucy stood on her tiptoes and looked up at the top of the globe. "What about North America?"

"You can't see it from down here," Tom said. "You have to climb on top. Want to try? You could walk around the world."

"I don't know," Lucy said. "Isn't it dangerous? Wouldn't I fall off?"

"Not if you do as I tell you," Tom said. "First, you have to climb up this metal thing that holds up the globe."

"Tom," said Lucy, "have *you* ever done this?"

"Sure, lots of times," said Tom. "Try it! It's fun — you'll see." He reached up and stopped the spinning globe.

Lucy grabbed hold of the band of curved metal and pulled herself up. She wrapped her legs around it and shinnied up to the North Pole. Then she was on top of the world. "Hey, Tom! I'm ready!" she yelled down.

"Okay," said Tom. "I'll start turning the globe. You just keep walking as it goes by under you, and always stay toward the top — that way you won't fall off."

"I'm all set," said Lucy. "Go slow, okay?"

"One more thing!" Tom yelled. "No fair walking on water."

"Oh, oh!" said Lucy. Then, "Oh, I see."

Tom set the globe spinning slowly. "Did you get wet?"

Lucy laughed. "Nope," she said. "I jumped over the English Channel to England then over to Iceland and then to Canada."

"Hooray!" Tom said. "You made it over the hardest part."

"Here comes Alaska," said Lucy.

Then she said, "I'm back where I

started from, Tom! I *really* have walked around the whole world."

Tom stopped the globe. He stopped it a little too quickly.

"*Ooops!*" said Lucy. She laughed. "I almost fell right in the middle of the North Sea!"

Lucy slid down from the globe. When she got to the table, she said, "I feel sorry for the big kids who come to the third grade."

"Oh, Lucy!" said Tom. "Didn't you think that was fun? Don't tell me you still hate the place."

"That's not what I meant," said Lucy. "I was just thinking how big kids can never walk around the globe the way we can."

Then the children spotted another strange-looking poster. They ran over to look at it.

"Let me read this one," said Lucy. "CAN YOU GUESS WHO MADE THESE TRACKS?"

"It's a bunch of animal tracks," said Tom. "Isn't it neat?"

"Look!" said Lucy. She pointed to a set of tracks on the poster. "We know those — they're raccoon tracks. Remember last summer when we saw the raccoon tracks, Tom?"

"Lucy," said Tom. He was grinning. "Do you want to play a trick on the big kids?"

Lucy smiled.

Tom began running. "Follow me!" he said.

The two children ran to the edge of the table where there was a pencil sharpener.

Tom sat down on the table and took off his shoes. Lucy sat down next to her brother and took her shoes off too.

Tom walked around in his bare feet near the pencil sharpener.

Lucy did the same thing. "What are we doing this for?" she asked.

"Walk on your tiptoes back to the poster," said Tom, "and I'll show you."

As soon as the children got to the poster, Tom lay down on his back with his feet up in the air. Then he pressed his bare feet against the poster right next to some bird tracks. Now his footprints were on the board too.

"It's *pencil dust,*" laughed Tom. "It was on the table near the pencil sharpener."

"That's wonderful!" said Lucy. "They'll never guess." Then she too put her footprints on the poster next to Tom's.

After Tom and Lucy put their shoes back on, they sat side by side on the edge of the table, their feet dangling over the side.

"You know," Lucy said, "I'm beginning to like third grade. What else can we do?"

Tom thought for a moment. Then, "Follow me," he said, and walked toward the far end of the table. "If it's in the right place, I'm going to show you the best thing of all."

"What is it?" asked Lucy. She followed along behind her brother.

They came to a machine at the end of the table.

"Good!" said Tom. "It's aimed at the screen, and it's far enough away."

"Far enough away for *what*?" said Lucy. "Tom, what are you talking about?"

"We have to get up on top of this projector," said Tom.

"Projector?" Lucy said.

Tom began to climb up the machine. It stood about twenty inches high. "I'm going to show you what a couple of tiny people would look like if they were regular-sized people," he said.

"I'm not going anywhere until you stop being mysterious," said Lucy. She put her hands on her hips.

Tom stood on top of the machine. "It's called an opaque projector," he said. "Come on up. I'll show you how it works."

In a few moments Lucy was standing beside her brother.

Tom pointed to the wall about ten feet away. "Do you see that screen over there?" he said. "The teacher can use this machine to show students things on that screen."

"Oh!" said Lucy. "Like a movie?"

"Not exactly," said Tom. "For a movie you need film. This thing doesn't. It can project almost anything on the screen — pictures from books, maps, even coins and stamps. Anything that can fit on this glass." Tom lifted up a hinged cover and pointed to a square of glass on top of the projector.

Lucy said, "Tom, do you mean we'll really be able to see ourselves way over there on that screen?"

"Sure. I'll move the cover up a little higher. See, now there's plenty of room for us to fit on the glass underneath," said Tom.

"Let's go," said Lucy. "I can hardly wait to see myself big."

"You first," said Tom. "I'll push the ON switch."

Lucy got down on her stomach and rolled underneath the cover and onto the glass. She lay on her back.

"You have to lie on your tummy," said Tom. "That way the lens in the machine can see the front of you."

Lucy flipped over. "Ready," she said.

"Look at the screen and squint your eyes," said Tom. "The light is kind of bright at first."

"All set, Tom," said Lucy, when she was ready.

Tom turned on the projector light. Instead of a tiny girl not quite four inches tall, there was an almost four-foot Lucy Little on the screen.

When Lucy got used to the bright light, she saw her image. "Tom, is that *me*?" she said.

"Wiggle your arms and legs," said Tom.

Lucy moved her body. "It *is* me!" she squealed. "But I can't see my face — only under my chin."

"That's because your head isn't facing the lens," said Tom.

Lucy lowered her head a bit, and at the same time kept her eyes on the screen.

"*There* I am!" she said. "Watch me dance, Tom." The tiny girl moved her arms and legs and hummed a tune.

Just then the schoolroom door swung open. Two night watchmen rushed into the room. One of the men called out, "Who's in here?"

Tom flicked off the projector light. Quickly, Lucy rolled out from under the cover. She and Tom climbed down from the machine. They ran and hid behind a pile of books on the table just as the schoolroom lights came on.

"Did you see what I saw?" asked the taller man.

"Yeah, a light — yeah!" said the other man.

"Not just a light — a girl on that screen over there," said the tall man.

"I didn't see no kid," said the second man. "Are you sure?"

"Sure I'm sure!"

"Was it from this here projector?" The second man put his hand on the projector. "Hey, yeah! It's still warm!"

"Someone must have been messing with this projector," whispered the tall man. "They must still be here — hiding."

The second man pointed to the other

end of the room. "That closet is the only place big enough to hide in," he said. "Let's rush it!"

"Let's go!" shouted the tall man. The men ran toward the closet.

Tom and Lucy slid down the table leg to the floor.

"Tom," said Lucy, "the secret door. It's over there where those men are!"

"C'mon, Lucy!" said Tom. "I know where there's another one." The tiny children dashed across the room and under a radiator. Tom found the door and pulled it open.

The children ran through the door.

"*Oomph!*" said Tom.

"*Ouch!*" said a voice.

Tom had run right into someone standing inside the wall passageway!

It was Cousin Dinky. Della was with him.

Cousin Dinky picked himself up off the floor. "Well, Tom," he said, "you pack a mean wallop." He rubbed his backside.

"Are you kids all right?" asked Della.

Tom looked at Lucy. They could see now. Dinky had turned on the lights. "Sure, we're okay," he said. "But where did you —?"

"We were looking all over the school for you," said Cousin Dinky.

"How did you know we were here?" Tom asked.

"Your Grandpa figured it out."

"We thought no one knew where we were," said Lucy.

"When you didn't show up," Cousin Dinky told them, "they looked in Henry's room and saw that the gerbils' cage was gone. Then everybody panicked. They thought for sure you were on your way to the Animal Hospital."

"But then," Della went on, "Grandpa said, 'Let's do something smart for a change.' "

Tom grinned. "That sounds like Grandpa."

"He looked at today's date on Mrs. Bigg's appointment calendar," Cousin Dinky said.

"And there it was in plain English," said Della. *Take Henry's gerbils to Mrs. White's second-grade class.*"

"They finally got a message to us late in the day," said Cousin Dinky. "We flew right over to the school and started looking for you."

"Oh, Della," said Lucy, giving her a big hug. "I'm so glad you found us."

Later, after visiting for a few minutes with Miss Gogg in her apartment, the Littles flew home. Lucy told everyone in the family that she loved school. "I'm not afraid to go anymore," she said. "I can hardly wait."

The day before Lucy and Tom were to join the other tiny children in school, a letter came from the author of *We Lived With Giants*. Henry Bigg couldn't understand why she sent a letter to him.

Tom and Lucy were listening when he read the letter to his mother:

Dear Henry,

Thank you for writing to me. I'm glad to hear that you enjoyed my book. I like your suggestion of writing a book about tiny people. I don't agree with you, however, that they should have tails. Nobody would ever believe that.

Sincerely,
Boa T. Rice